A TROUBLESOME CREEK
Kids Story

Trouble in
Troublesome Creek

Story by
Nancy Kelly Allen

Illustrated by
K. Michael Crawford

A Red Pebble Book

from Red Rock Press

for Sterling

— Nancy Kelly Allen

for my family,
hoping all your creeks stay trouble free

— K. Michael Crawford

Trouble in Troublesome Creek

The volume you are holding is made of recycled materials.

This book, including illustrations, may not be copied in whole or part by any means without the express permission of Red Rock Press. Queries may be directed to info@redrockpress.com.

Text copyright © 2010 Nancy Kelly Allen
Illustrations copyright © 2010 K. Michael Crawford

ISBN 978-1-933176-36-9

Design by Susan Smilanic of Studio 21, Durango CO

Published by Red Rock Press of Telluride CO and New York NY

Red Rock Press
459 Columbus Avenue
New York   New York 10024

www.RedRockPress.com

Library of Congress Cataloging-in-Publication Data

Allen, Nancy Kelly, 1949-
  Trouble in Troublesome Creek : a Troublesome Creek kids story / by Nancy
Kelly Allen ; [illustrations by K. Michael Crawford].
      p. cm.
  Summary: When dead fish are discovered in a favorite swimming hole, the
Troublesome Creek gang decides to investigate.
  ISBN 978-1-933176-32-1 (alk. paper)
 [1. Water--Pollution--Fiction.] I. Crawford, K. Michael, ill. II. Title
  PZ7.A4318Tr 2010
  [E]--dc22
                              2009018470

Printed in Hong Kong, China

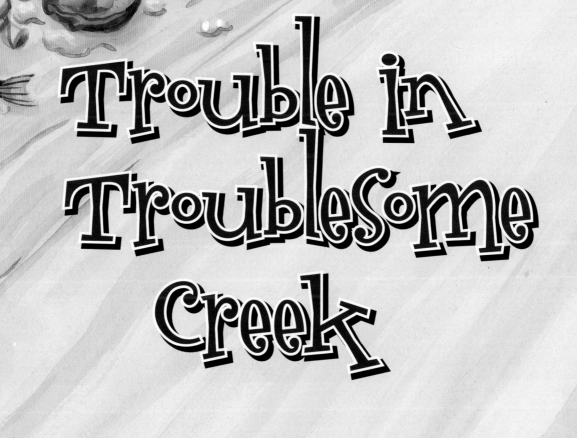

Trouble in Troublesome Creek

Story by
Nancy Kelly Allen

Illustrated by
K. Michael Crawford

Trouble was floating in Troublesome Creek. Dean pinched his nose. His big sister Liz hollered, "Dead fish in the water!" Dean whooped, "Whooooowee!"

Liz eyeballed Dean. "Whooooowee" was *her* special scream. Meanwhile, know-it-all Sallie stuck a swift elbow to my ribs. "Five. No, six floaters," she gloated, as if no one else could count. "See 'em, James? Stinnnnky!"

"I thought that smell was your feet," I answered as I scooped a dead fish out of the water with a long stick. Quiet, careful Carolyn shrank back.

Sallie asked, "*Who* killed the fish just so we couldn't swim?"

I hadn't thought of that. Was this fish murder and not an accident?

I looked around and saw that Aunt Pearl, in one of her old straw hats, had come out to weed in the razzle-dazzle community garden above our swimming hole. She was tidying the red-white-and-blue flowerbed in the shape of Old Glory. Maybe Aunt Pearl would know what to do or if it was safe to swim. But asking her was dangerous. She might put us to work.

I worked up my nerve as we walked over. "Aunt Pearl," I said, "you deserve a blue ribbon, like the one Liz won for her flowers last summer."

Sallie piped up, "Only *one* blue ribbon? *I've* won four."

Aunt Pearl ignored Miss Know-It-All, smiled and thanked me. Then I told her about the floating fish.

"Oh, my," Aunt Pearl exclaimed. "It's truly a mystery." She shook her head. "Now you wouldn't still be thinking of *swimming* in Troublesome Creek?"

We skedaddled back to the ooh-ah rope tied to an oak branch. Instead of a splashdown in the water with dead fish—yuck!—we decided we'd swing wide and land on the soggy sand of the opposite bank.

My hands bare-fisted the rope. But I was too jumpy to jump. So I stood there, still as a pine tree.

Sallie sneered, "You're a nervous pervous, James Hicks."

I showed her as I shot out and yelled "Oooooh!"
As I landed, my gang sang, "Ahhhhhh!"
Every morning for two weeks 'cept one day when it was raining like crashing arrows, we checked out our swimming hole.

Every morning 'cept the one when we didn't look, we found more dead fish. Every day we looked, four of us—Liz, Dean, Carolyn and me—asked the same question: *What's* causing the fish to die? And Sallie asked, "*Who* is causing the fish to die?"

We also asked everyone we saw.

Everyone had the same answer:

I don't know.

One morning, I grabbed the ooh-ah rope and flew over the creek but my hands slipped and I crash-landed on the hill on the other side of the stream. Rocks tumbled. My wobbly knees wobbled more when I gazed down a big hole. The mountain had gaped open like a yawn.

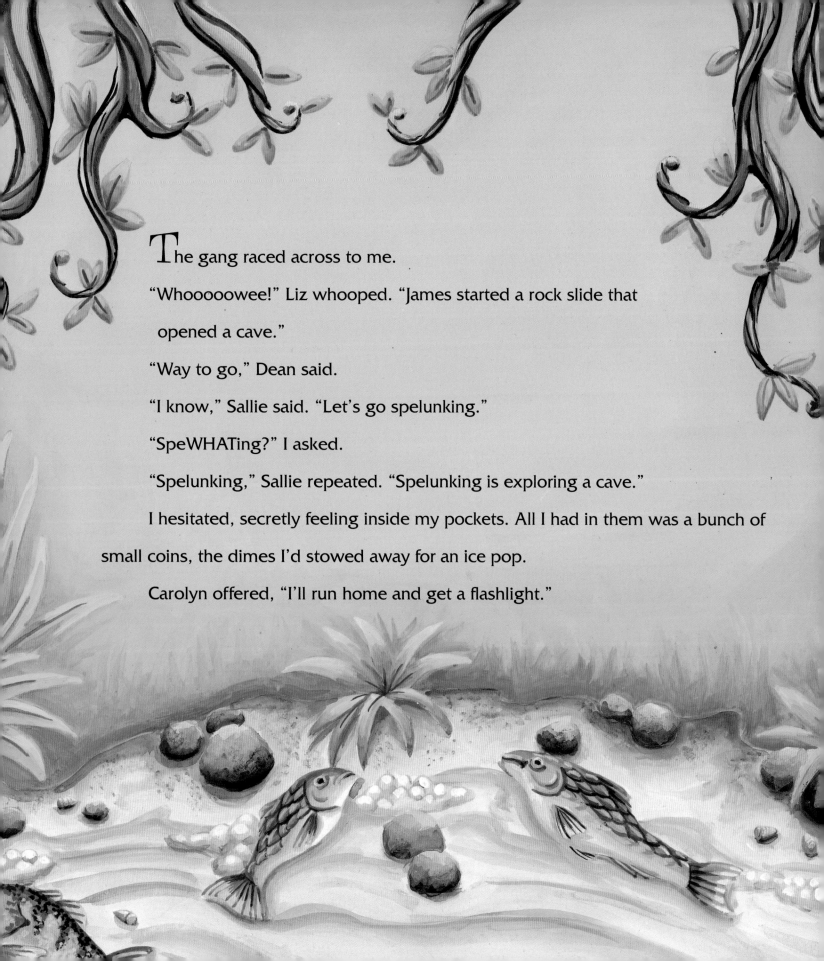

The gang raced across to me.

"Whoooowee!" Liz whooped. "James started a rock slide that opened a cave."

"Way to go," Dean said.

"I know," Sallie said. "Let's go spelunking."

"SpeWHATing?" I asked.

"Spelunking," Sallie repeated. "Spelunking is exploring a cave."

I hesitated, secretly feeling inside my pockets. All I had in them was a bunch of small coins, the dimes I'd stowed away for an ice pop.

Carolyn offered, "I'll run home and get a flashlight."

Faster than two shakes of a lamb's tail Carolyn was back, bound for action. She started onward and downward, and we trailed her through twists and turns in the deep, dark tunnels that plowed through the mountain.

Cold air goose-bumped my goose bumps. I stuck my hands back in my pockets to see if I had any dimes left. Something nearly swooped into my head. "Yikes!" I called out as bats swarmed us.

"We'll be bat burgers," Sallie yelped. She bolted her hands to my arm and we slid into Carolyn whose flashlight thumped on the ground, flickered and shut off.

Pitch black swallowed us whole. My hand rubbed against a pile of small rocks. Shaking, I swished my hand on the ground, grabbed up the flashlight, and flicked it. Didley squat. I shook it twice, and we had light. Whew! I pointed the light toward the rocks. *They were strange.*

"What are they?" Dean asked.

"Beats me," I answered. I handed Carolyn her flashlight and picked up a sample. "This isn't stone. It's some kind of metal."

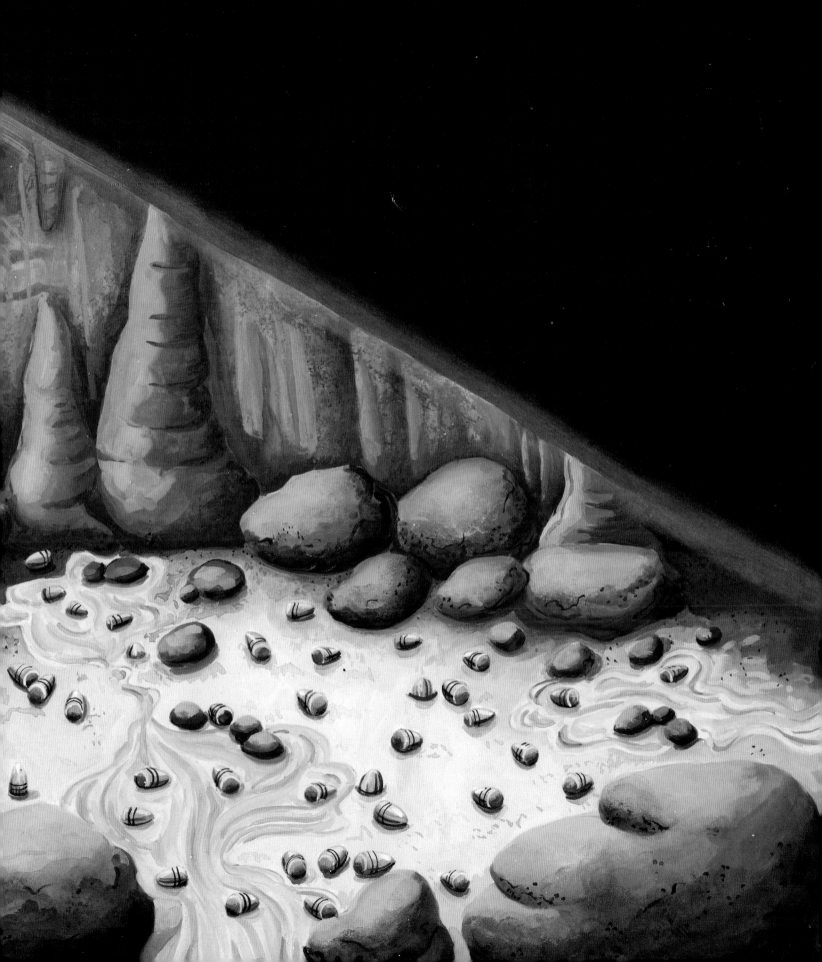

Carolyn whipped the light around the cave.
Bats flapped and fluttered. We ducked and dodged.

"Forget the rocks," Sallie said. "Let's rip out of here."

"Anyone remember the way?" Carolyn asked.
Liz pointed right. Sallie pointed left. Dean

stuck his thumb in his mouth.

"It's okay," I said. "I kept track of our route

with dimes. Three turns left, one right, and two

more left turns should take us to the

opening. But we gotta keep the flashlight

pointed down."

Flapping bats

spilled shivers down my

spine,   but we plugged on,

tracing back to the second dime

I'd dropped. I crunched to pick it up. "One more left

turn," I said.

"Whooooowee! Sunshine!" Liz squealed.

She and Dean scrambled out of the cave.

Near the cave opening, I eyed more metal rocks. They were covered in water.

That afternoon we carried some metal pebbles to the Troublesome Creek Museum. The director examined them and said they were really Civil War bullets called minnie balls. He showed us a short movie about the War that had minnie balls in it. Minnie balls were made of lead, the director said. He thought minnie balls might stay dangerous for a long time because lead is poisonous.

Poisonous! I wondered if the minnie balls were poisoning the water and fish.

The museum director asked us to show him the cave, and he gave us each a powerful flashlight. On the way we saw Aunt Pearl watering the begonias. "Aunt Pearl! Come here quick!" Liz called out.

Some minutes later, Aunt Pearl leaned into the cave with us. "I don't mind a tad more dirt," Aunt Pearl said. "I'm already wearing sweet garden soil." I pointed to the batch of minnie balls not far from inside the cave. "Do tell!" Aunt Pearl said. "My granddaddy always told me that Confederate soldiers holed up in a cave along here. I declare, I thought his story was farfetched—until now."

The museum director arranged another meeting. The next morning we took a county water official to the swimming hole and then crossed the bridge to show her the cave.

Four days later, the *Troublesome Creek Caller* had the story. A picture on the front page showed the cave with a heap of minnie balls outside it. *Who moved our minnie balls?* I don't know. But, sure enough, the paper said the minnie balls were leaking lead into the cave water which was leaking lead into our swimming hole. There was also a photo of dead fish.

In the story, the museum director credited us with discovering the long lost cave. But he didn't call out our names. He just described us as the "Troublesome Creek Gang." I liked that.

Liz read aloud the description of our gang: "A spunky group of local youngsters, smart enough to suspect they'd found something important."

"They should've put in *my* name," Sallie said, all pouty-like.

Liz flipped the page and asked, "Can you believe it? A war that was fought almost a century and a half ago is killing our fish today."

Carolyn thought a bit and said, "I've heard that kids around the world get hurt from the leftovers of war. An old, unexploded bomb goes off or someone steps on a mine."

Dean clutched Liz.

Sallie perked up, proclaiming. "Oprah will want us on her show."

I was confused.

"Duh-uh," Sallie said. "We're heroes. We could have been blown up!"

Tears popped into Dean's eyes.

"Don't be such a drama queen," Liz snapped at Sallie. "The only things endangered here are the fish."

"More than that," I muttered. "The fish are dead, and our swimming hole is gone for good."

But I was wrong. Three Fridays later, the Troublesome Creek swimming hole was pronounced clean and officially reopened. Since no one had actually bothered to close it, officials had to put up orange tape to cut. We attended the reopening in our bathing suits.

As soon as the county people and the photographer left, Liz hollered,

"Whoooooowee! What are we waiting for?"

Back on the hillside, I bare-fisted the ooh-ah rope, ready to shoot out and drop feet first into the water. Then, I froze.

"Nervoooous Pervoooous!" Sallie yelled.

So I sailed out and let go.